of Eggs

Copyright Information

THE CLUTCH OF EGGS
by Debbie Young
© Debbie Young 2020
Published by Hawkesbury Press 2020
Hawkesbury Upton, Gloucestershire
Cover design by Rachel Lawston of Lawston Design

ISBN (paperback) 978-1-911223-64-1

About the Author

Debbie Young writes warm, witty, feel-good fiction. All her novels are set in the Cotswolds, the beautiful rural region of the West of England where she has lived most of her adult life.

Her Sophie Sayers Village Mystery series runs the course of a year in the fictional Cotswold village of Wendlebury Barrow and now includes a growing number of shorter stories, Tales from Wendlebury Barrow.

Her Staffroom at St Bride's series takes place just down the road from Sophie's village, and in some stories characters from both series meet.

Her humorous short stories are available in themed collections, such as *Marry in*

Haste, *Quick Change* and *Stocking Fillers*, and in many anthologies.

She is a frequent speaker at literature festivals and writers' events and is founder and director of the free Hawkesbury Upton Literature Festival. She is often a guest on BBC Radio Gloucestershire's Book Club.

A regular contributor to two local community magazines, the award-winning *Tetbury Advertiser* and the *Hawkesbury Parish News*, she has published two collections of her columns, *Young by Name* and *All Part of the Charm*. These publications offer insight into her personal life and make interesting companion pieces to her fiction.

For the latest information about Debbie Young's books and events, visit her Writing Life website, where you may also like to join her free Readers' Club
www.authordebbieyoung.com

To Tim Birkhead, Andy Holden
and Peter Holden
for awakening me
to the wonder of eggs

"I think that,
if required on pain of death
to name instantly
the most perfect thing in the universe,
I should risk my fate on a bird's egg."
Thomas Wentworth Higginson

"An egg is just egg-shaped, isn't it?
Hence the name."
Sophie Sayers

The Clutch of Eggs

Tales from Wendlebury Barrow

Debbie Young

1 The Foundling Egg

"Look at this, Hector!"

I held out my hand to reveal what I'd carried so carefully all the way from my cottage to Hector's House, the village bookshop.

Instead of giving me my usual morning hug before flipping the door sign to "open", Hector (my boyfriend as well as my boss) stood back in awe of the object's fragility.

"What's that, your breakfast? It's a bit on the small side. You're not on a diet, are you?"

I stroked the pristine white shell with my fingertip.

"No, silly, it's a bird's egg. What sort of monster do you take me for? I don't eat birds' eggs for breakfast. Apart from hens' eggs, I mean."

I was glad I'd had toast that morning instead.

"That's no hen's egg. It's far too small. Did you get it from the village shop? I'd heard Carol had started stocking quails' eggs, but I thought they were speckled."

"Yes, she has, and they are. She's thrilled to have something to put on her Q shelf at last." Carol organises her stock alphabetically to make things easier to find. "But I've no idea what sort of bird laid this egg."

Hector slipped his hand into his pocket and pulled out the key to his flat above the bookshop.

"I'll fetch the vintage *Observer's Book of Birds' Eggs* from my curiosities collection upstairs. That'll help us identify it."

He turned the door sign to "open" before dashing outside and disappearing round the corner of the shop.

"What if it's not a vintage bird?" I called after him, but his footsteps were already pounding up the stairs to his flat.

I like to tease Hector about the funny old books that fill his spare bedroom. He's never read most of them, he just likes the look and feel of them. I can't understand why he doesn't add a second-hand department to the shop. He'd have more than enough stock, and it would provide a useful source of extra income for the business. We're always looking for new income streams. It's not easy keeping a rural bookshop in profit.

The sun was shining brightly now, so, still cradling the egg with my spare hand, I propped the door open with our cast-iron doorstop, which is shaped like a pile of old books. The fresh spring air was full of the scent of new leaves, the shrubs and trees along the high street acid green with new growth. I lingered on the threshold for a deep breath before going back inside, where I gently set my egg on the trade counter to await Hector's verdict. To make sure it wouldn't roll away and fall on the floor, I surrounded it with a little wall of stationery.

As Hector's footsteps thundered back down the stairs, I headed for the tearoom, which is my domain, and fired up the coffee machine. We always start our working day with a caffeine fix. The smell of fresh coffee helps lure our first customers in off the street, too – mums returning from the school run.

Hector strode back into the shop brandishing a small hardback with a plain tan cover. Taking his usual seat at the trade counter, he started to flick through its yellowing pages. He didn't look up when I set down in front of him a tiny espresso cup branded with *The Birds* by Daphne du Maurier. My wit was wasted on him. To be fair, the book he was reading was engrossing. On almost every page there was a precise and beautiful watercolour illustration of a bird's egg, each one different.

"Surprisingly few eggs seem to be plain white like yours. Or the same shape."

I gazed at the egg nestling in its pen of pens.

"Surely it's just egg-shaped? Hence the expression."

He held the book up to show me.

"This one's the right colour, but it's longer and thinner than your egg, while this one is more rounded." He paused at the swift's page. "The swift's is plain white, but it's too long."

"Isn't it too early for a swift, anyway?"

"Yes, you're right. They won't arrive for another week or two yet." He flicked through a few more pages. The lesser-spotted woodpecker lays small white eggs the right shape, but I doubt you've got a woodpecker in your garden. They're a bit shy and more of a forest dweller. Besides, it says here they don't start laying till May." He looked up from the book. "You did find this egg in your garden, didn't you?"

I beamed with pride.

"I didn't. Blossom did. She brought it in to me this morning. Isn't she clever?" Blossom is my kitten. Hector's not keen on cats, but I thought this show of skill might raise her in his

5

estimation. "Do you realise how gentle Blossom must have been to pick up something as fragile as an egg in her mouth without breaking it? To carry it all the way from wherever she found it to my kitchen? I think she meant it as a present for me."

Hector moved the book closer to his eyes. The print was tiny. Encouraged by his silence, I continued.

"At first, I thought she'd squashed her ping-pong ball, but no. It's as perfect an egg as you'll find anywhere in nature."

Hector harrumphed. "I just hope Blossom didn't despatch the mother bird while she was at her nest." He shot me a mournful look. "Although that would cut short the mother's distress at losing her egg."

A wave of vicarious guilt swept over me.

"There aren't any nests in my garden," I began, despite realising I hadn't actually checked. Might nests be hidden among the fresh spring foliage? My dense evergreens would also provide perfect camouflage.

6

Our conversation was cut short by a hum of chatter approaching from the direction of the school, so Hector set down the book to continue his investigations later.

A chilly breeze struck up as the school run-mums arrived. Although reluctant to shut out the spring, I closed the door behind them.

It was only when I was starting to serve their coffee that I realised Hector hadn't given me my morning hug.

2 Sina's Surprise

The clang of the village primary school bell for the end of lessons carried down the high street on the fresh breeze, and moments later, the bookshop door flew open to admit one of its older pupils, Sina. Not bothering to close the door behind her, she ran into the middle of the shop and held her right hand up to make an announcement.

"Look what I've just found, Hector! Sophie, look what I've found. I found it just now in the playpark. Look, Billy! Look –" She hesitated, keen to get the attention of the other customers in the shop, but not knowing them by name. "Look, everybody!"

She held out her left hand, palm upwards, and uncurled her fingers to reveal a tiny, perfect egg, the identical twin of the one Blossom had brought me.

Her older brother Tommy, fresh from the senior school bus, appeared in the doorway, his hands in his trouser pockets. Maybe fresh is the wrong word. His school tie hung awry, his blazer was crumpled and his trousers muddy, although it hadn't rained for days.

"Actually, I found that egg. And now I'm off to look for another one. I'm thinking of starting a collection."

Then he strolled off in the direction of the churchyard.

A tall wiry man emerged from the fiction section to address Sina.

"Found it? I'm afraid he means he stole it. Don't you know it's illegal to take wild birds' eggs from their nests? Has been for years. Removing it from its natural habitat counts as theft."

Sina, still cradling her egg in her left hand, put her right hand on her hip in indignation.

"Are you calling my brother a thief? If so, that must make Carol a thief too, because she sells eggs in her shop. Don't you call my brother a thief, nor Carol neither."

Tommy was often a source of annoyance to Sina, but when challenged she was deeply loyal to him.

Puzzled, the man looked to me as the nearest member of staff for explanation. Realising he wasn't from Wendlebury Barrow, I came to his rescue.

"Carol runs the village shop, sir. Sina, 'wild' is the key word here. Carol sells only the eggs of domesticated birds. Collecting eggs from farmed chickens is not only allowed, it's encouraged."

Sina frowned. "What about those little tiny eggs she's selling now, the spotty ones?"

"They're quails' eggs, but the quails are farmed, same as the hens."

Sina cupped both hands around her egg.

"Well, anyhow, Tommy didn't steal my egg. He found it on the ground. The bird can't have wanted it if it just left it there. It had probably flown south for the winter, like birds do."

She parted her hands just enough to allow the stranger a closer look at the egg.

"But it's spring. And woodpigeons don't fly south at any time of year. Woodpigeons stay put. That's definitely a woodpigeon's egg."

"Ah, woodpigeon!" murmured Hector, looking it up in the *Observer's Book* index.

"More likely the egg had fallen from the nest," the stranger continued. "Did you find it underneath a tree? The mother may have inadvertently knocked it overboard when she went to look for food. Or she may have recognised it was unfertilised and discarded it on purpose."

Sina seized the chance of an alibi for her brother.

"Yes, that'll be it. Tommy wasn't stealing it, he was tidying up, like people do after their dogs. Just doing a good turn as he was passing by."

12

Hector laid down his bird book and sat back to savour the conversation.

"Are you sure he wasn't just passing *through* the tree? He climbs trees like a monkey, that boy."

Sina ignored him. "Or maybe it was just a lazy bird that couldn't be bothered to build a nest and decided to lay its egg on the ground. Or it might have got caught short while it was out, really needing to lay its egg, and couldn't make it back to the nest in time. That's happened to me before while I've been out on a long walk. Well, not laying eggs, but you know what I mean."

A couple of customers browsing the health and well-being section sniggered. Even the stranger was struggling to look stern.

"That's not the same thing at all. But thank you for reminding me that I actually came in to collect a book about birds' eggs I ordered online from you the other day." He headed to the trade counter. "Has it come in yet, please?"

Hector located it on the Specials shelf, where I'd put it after unpacking the morning's deliveries. I remembered now that I hadn't recognised the customer's name on the order form, and I'd wondered who he was.

I was about to find out.

3 The Bird Man
Of Wendlebury Barrow

As Hector engaged the stranger in conversation, Sina headed for the tearoom, hoping I'd be more sympathetic. She was luckier than she'd dared hope. Nestling in one of the small wicker baskets I use for serving scones was her egg's exact twin. She lay hers down in the basket beside it.

"Snap!" She turned to call across to the stranger at the counter. "You see, Sophie's got one too, so it must be all right."

I went to set a pot of tea down in front of old Billy, who grinned at me.

"I didn't have you down as a tree climber, girlie. Has that young Tommy been leading you astray?"

I laughed as I went back behind the counter. "Not me, Billy. I don't even like standing on a chair to change a lightbulb. No, my cat Blossom brought me this egg this morning."

Billy tutted. "Ah, well, that's cats for you. Killers, ruthless killers, the lot of them."

This was a bit rich, considering Billy had given me Blossom in the first place.

As I started to empty the dishwasher, Sina touched my egg with her fingertip.

"So what are you going to do with your egg, Sophie? I thought I might try to hatch mine."

"I don't think that will work once the egg gets cold."

She put the back of her hand to each egg, then pointed to the microwave.

"How about we warm them up in there?"

I spluttered. "Goodness, no, that'll just cook them."

Her face fell. Like her brother, she generally meant well.

"Maybe Hector's new friend over there can suggest something." I nodded towards the trade counter, where Hector was slipping one of the shop's promotional bookmarks into the stranger's purchase.

Hearing his name, Hector addressed his customer. "I think Sophie is after your advice, Michael."

"It'll be a pleasure." Michael strolled over to the tearoom with the easy lope of a practised rambler. "But I'm afraid I'm more of a birdwatcher than an eggwatcher. If you were to ask me which came first, I'd say the chicken."

I smiled. Perhaps he wasn't so bad after all. "Are you stopping for a coffee? Or afternoon tea?"

I didn't want to upset Sina by encouraging him to linger, but unlike Sina, he was a paying customer.

Michael pulled back the sleeve of his jacket to check a chunky black watch, the sort that tells you your elevation, the air pressure, and the times around the world.

"Cappuccino time, on the dot." He straightened his cuff. "After all, I am on holiday. I might even make a start on my new book."

He showed me the cover, replete with simple but stunning images of birds' eggs in shades of cream and blue, their shells mottled with dark flecks and inky squiggles.

"Wow, they're like works of art."

Sina leaned forward and narrowed her eyes.

"Or messages in secret code."

She went to collect a pencil and paper from the children's play table before sitting down beside Michael, uninvited.

"Hector, can I please borrow your egg book so I can draw some nice eggs?" she called across the shop.

Hector, always keen to encourage young readers, brought it across and laid it on the table in front of her, open at a page showing highly patterned eggs. With a confident flourish, she drew an egg shape and began to cover it in swirls and splashes.

When I delivered Michael's cappuccino, I took the wicker scone basket of eggs to his table to show him.

"The eggs on the cover of your book make our eggs look a bit dull."

"Not at all. There's a lovely technical term for pure white eggs: immaculate."

I smiled. "How poetic."

"People are often surprised to learn that even some of the most glamorous-looking birds lay immaculate eggs. The peacock, for example. Egg colour doesn't relate to the bird's plumage. Instead, it reflects its habitat. Plain eggs usually come from birds that nest in safe places, where camouflage isn't necessary to deter predators."

"I expect you've seen a lot of woodpigeons' eggs out birdwatching. Or are you only interested in seeing rare birds in unexpected places?"

He shook his head. "I'm no twitcher."

19

Sina glanced up from her drawing to give him a funny look. He understood her confusion at once.

"In this context, Sina, a twitcher doesn't mean someone with a twitch. It means the sort of birdwatcher who will dash off to anywhere in the country to sight an unusual bird. There's also an app called Twitcher that publicises reports of rare birds so that interested twitchers can flock to see them, if you'll pardon the pun." He paused to take a sip of his cappuccino. "I'm more of a birder. That means I stick to my home patch, rather than dashing around the country to tick a new bird off my watch list. Having said that, I'm always happy to find new ones when I'm away on holiday. Last summer, I saw the famous ospreys at Loch Garten."

"Ooh, ospreys!" I felt on firmer ground now. "I've seen ospreys near Loch Ness where my parents live."

Eavesdropping at the next table, Billy chortled.

"Look out, Hector, you could end up with a monster for a mother-in-law."

I wasn't sure whether Hector was grimacing at Billy's profile of my mum or at the suggestion of marriage. We were nowhere near ready to talk about marriage yet.

"My parents don't live in Loch Ness, Billy. They're to its north in Inverness, just by the river. The River Ness runs north from Loch Ness, through Loch Dochfour, then up to Inverness. I think the ospreys are in the woodland on the shore of Loch Dochfour."

Billy rattled his cup as he set it down on his saucer, having missed the indent in the middle. I keep telling him he ought to wear the glasses he keeps in the top pocket of his jacket. How he's never got run over crossing the road is beyond me.

"I didn't come in here for a geography lesson, girlie."

Before I could respond, Tommy, trousers now streaked with moss and lichen, burst in, almost knocking over the elderly lady Hector

21

was serving at the trade counter. Tommy bounded over to Michael's table, where Sina was still drawing.

"You got my egg, Sina? I hope you haven't broken it. I couldn't find any others just now, but I'm going out egg hunting again tomorrow after school. I'm going to make a whole new section on birds' eggs in my museum."

Laying down her pencil, Sina rolled her eyes at me. "He means his birds' nest of a bedroom, Sophie." Then she gazed wide-eyed at her brother as if he couldn't have heard what she'd just said to me. "Oh, Tommy, I thought you'd given that dear little egg to me. Besides, you know I can look after an egg much better than you can. You know you'll only break it, like you did that skellington."

I didn't like to ask whose skeleton it was or where he'd found it.

To avert a quarrel, I stepped between them, holding out my wicker basket.

"Here, you can have my egg, Sina. I don't really have a use for it. Then you'll have one each. But no more collecting, Tommy. It's a crime to take birds' eggs from the wild, whether from the nest or even if you just find them on the ground. Got that? A crime."

As Tommy shrugged, Sina shot to her feet. When they both reached for the basket at once, I expected the eggs to end up scrambled.

"You can keep the basket," I said quickly. "I can't use it for scones again now. It would be unhygienic."

Tommy snatched it from me and hugged it to his chest, while Sina, looking around for a trophy of her own, picked up Hector's vintage book of birds' eggs. She shot me a questioning glance.

"Well, he did say I could borrow it. My brother might like to look at it too. I'll bring it back when we're done. It's only a borrow."

As Hector was now on the phone to a supplier, I said yes on his behalf. I didn't think he'd mind.

Once Tommy and Sina had fled, arguing about which egg was whose, the shop felt strangely quiet. Then Billy broke the silence by lifting the lid of his teapot and peering inside, his customary hint for a free refill.

Michael scraped back his chair. "Well, I suppose I'd better be heading off, Sophie, thank you." He dropped a few coins beneath his saucer as a tip. I always feel uncomfortable receiving tips from good-looking men.

"Will we see you again before the end of your holiday?" I asked to cover my embarrassment.

"Maybe, although at this rate I suspect this book will keep me going till I go home." Thanks to the floor show by Tommy and Sina, he hadn't managed to get beyond the first page. "Still, nice meeting you."

He bade Hector a friendly goodbye as he headed for the door.

4 Eggy by Name

Billy settled back in his chair as I topped up his teapot with hot water.

"You know, girlie, I used to be a bit of a birdwatcher when I were a lad. Even collected the odd egg meself. In those days it weren't illegal, but I didn't go in for it as much as some. Hunting for wild birds' nests weren't no novelty to me, as collecting the eggs from our fowls was one of my chores. I had to clean out the henhouse every Saturday, too, and that put me right off 'em. I just associated birds' eggs with muck on me boots and ammonia in me lungs. You ever been inside a henhouse, girlie? It's like a shed full of smelling salts."

"Ugh, sounds horrid."

"My cousin Eggy, now, he was mad for collecting eggs. Wild birds' eggs, I mean. His mum, my Auntie Emily, never kept fowls, as my mum gave her our surplus. Swapped 'em for a share in her pig when it was killed."

"Your cousin was called Eggy? There's a fine case of nominative determinism." He looked blank. "Growing into your name, I mean. What was his full name, Egbert?"

It was the only boy's name I could think of that might be shortened to Eggy.

"No, it was Albert. I was more of a conker boy myself. Mind you, we took whatever we found into school for the nature table – eggs, birds' nests, conkers, leaf skeletons, sticklebacks, the lot. You could have built whole animals from the relics we brought in each term. Not all from the same animal, of course."

"You mean like Frankenstein's monster?" I grimaced. "Don't tell Tommy. You'll give him ideas."

Having hit a quiet spell on the trade counter, Hector came over to help himself to a snack.

"Your poor teacher must have had a strong stomach." He selected a flapjack from under a glass dome and took a hearty bite.

"We had a sheep's stomach once," said Billy. "One of the farmers' boys brought it in for a bit of fun. That's when the teacher decided to get rid of the nature table to make way for a new reading corner."

Hector sat down in the empty chair at Billy's table. "A teacher after my own heart."

"I can tell you a very funny story about a pig's bladder," began Billy, at which point I pleaded an urgent need to go to the stockroom, where I lurked until he'd finished.

I hoped neither the flapjack nor the anecdote would spoil Hector's appetite for dinner at my house that evening.

5 Q is for Quail

"I see you've bought some of Carol's new line."

Too curious to mind my manners, I peered into Kate's wicker shopping basket at a pair of transparent plastic boxes filled with tiny speckled eggs. I'd bumped into Hector's godmother outside the village shop on my way home from work.

"Yes, isn't it marvellous, Sophie? Carol's just pinned down a local supplier."

I pictured Carol wrestling a female quail into submission.

Before I could reply, the bell above the shop door jangled, and Tommy charged out into the street. Kate waved her forefinger at him.

"If the wind changes, you'll be stuck with that frown forever."

"Don't care if I am," he retorted, but his scowl softened. Kate has that effect on people, lifting their spirits as she drifts about the village. She's the nearest thing Wendlebury has to a fairy godmother.

Then Tommy spotted what was in Kate's basket.

"You're lucky she let you have some of them. She wouldn't let me buy a single one. You don't have to be 18 to buy eggs, do you? It's not like eggs contain alcohol. What's the world suddenly got against eggs?"

Kate was more than equal to pacifying Tommy.

"If by 'she' you mean Carol, she can't have run out of quails' eggs already. There were still half a dozen boxes on the Q shelf after I'd bought these a few moments ago."

Tommy shuffled his feet.

"I don't want six boxes. I only want one egg. I don't ask much."

"Just one egg? That won't fill a growing boy like you. Goodness, even I can eat half a dozen quails' eggs at one sitting."

Tommy brightened.

"Have you ever seen egg-eating competitions on YouTube, Kate? Sophie, you and Hector are always saying you want to hold more events in your shop. Why don't you organise an egg-eating competition in your tearoom? You should go in for it, Kate. Although I bet I'd win, even if you have got a bigger belly than me."

Kate's free hand flew to her gently rounded stomach.

"It's only quails' eggs that I can eat in any quantity because they're so tiny. I couldn't eat more than one of any other sort of egg at a time. Apart from caviar, obviously."

Tommy shrugged. "You just need to train up gradually. You can use really little eggs to start with. Then each day just eat one more than the day before. It won't take long till you're champion standard. You'll never even

31

notice the difference. My mum does the same in reverse when she's cutting down on her pills. It's a good system."

"Thank you for your vote of confidence, Tommy, but I think I'll leave egg-eating competitions to the likes of you and Paul Newman. Anyway, back to the point. You can't expect Carol to split a box of quails' eggs to sell you a single one, any more than she'd open a bag of sweets to sell you one chocolate button. Quails' eggs are generally only sold in boxes of half a dozen or a dozen, same as hens' eggs. But I tell you what, you can have one of my eggs."

She reached into her basket to prise open an egg box and remove an egg.

"Here you go, Tommy, you can have this one on me as a treat, if you promise to pick up any litter you see on your way home."

Always pleased to have a mission, Tommy pulled a crumpled length of toilet paper from his blazer pocket, wrapped up the egg, and slipped it into his trouser pocket.

"Wow, thanks, mate." He flashed her a grateful smile before charging off down the street on litter patrol.

"Mate?" echoed Kate.

I laughed. "That's high praise, coming from Tommy."

Carefully, Kate resealed the egg box. "Well, that's my good deed for the day, and his too. I just hope his mother gives him something else to go with it for his supper. A growing lad like that must take some filling. I remember Hector's voracious appetite when he was Tommy's age."

I grinned. It was funny to think of Hector as a teenager.

"Believe it or not, Kate, for all Tommy's talk of egg-eating competitions, he's not planning to eat it. He wants it for his new collection. A collection of birds' eggs."

Kate's face fell.

"Oh, dear. That will never do. I wouldn't have let him have it if I'd known. You do know it's against the law to collect wild birds' eggs? I know the quail that laid these eggs isn't wild, but still…"

"Yes, of course, and so does he. I've told him in no uncertain terms. We need to divert him on to a different passion, preferably one that's legal."

Kate let out a trill of laughter.

"Good luck with that, Sophie! If I find any suitable openings, I'll let you know."

6 In a Stew

I was mashing the potatoes when a knock at the door announced Hector's arrival. We've never exchanged house keys – there's no need as everyone round here keeps a spare under a flowerpot near their front door, but even so, we respect each other's space by never barging in unannounced.

I scurried to the door, wiping my damp hands on my skirt as I went so as not to leave prints on him. As soon as he's inside the door and out of sight of the neighbours, he always gives me a bear hug.

Hug accomplished, he slipped off his waxed jacket and hung it on the peg that I keep free for him on the hallstand. I led the way through my small sitting room.

"Come through, dinner's just about ready."

As we entered the kitchen, a light patter on the stairs heralded Blossom's entrance. Oblivious to Hector's antipathy, she gave him a chirrup of welcome, rubbing her chin and neck against his ankles.

"Hello, child-killer," was his terse response.

"Oh, Hector, an egg is hardly the same as a child." As an antidote to his harsh words, I bent down to stroke the top of her head.

Hector settled into his usual pine carver dining chair opposite mine.

"Tell that to the poor mother bird. Why do you think collecting wild birds' eggs is illegal? If enough cats did it, they'd wipe out whole species."

"You can't expect Blossom to know that. She was just being a cat, doing what cats do. They're natural hunters."

Hector kicked off his shoes under the table. Blossom, her self-esteem inviolable, interpreted this gesture as an invitation to nuzzle his toes. He drew his feet up underneath him.

"That's just one reason I prefer dogs. At least dogs don't raid birds' nests."

For every reason he might state in favour of dogs, I could have cited two on the side of cats, but I wasn't about to play that game. Instead I distracted him by taking a bottle of Carol's best dry white wine from the fridge and passing it to him to open. He reached into his trouser pocket for his Swiss Army knife.

"Speaking of dogs," he continued as he unfolded the corkscrew attachment, "did you hear old Mrs Shipley has just had a hip replacement?"

As he twisted the curl of metal into the cork, I shared the mash between two plates.

"Who's Mrs Shipley?"

I donned thick gloves to lift the chicken casserole out of the oven. Hector shifted in his chair to return his feet to the floor and sat up straight, ready to eat.

"I don't suppose you've ever spoken to her. She's been a bit of a recluse since her husband died a few years ago. But you'd know her if you saw her. She only emerges from her cottage to walk her little dachshund, Bunty. Anyway, I bumped into Judy Parkinson, the health visitor, on the way here, and she mentioned Mrs Shipley is looking for a dog walker while she convalesces. Mrs Shipley's been letting Bunty out into her back garden, but she's fretting about the lack of proper walks."

As I removed the lid from the casserole dish, a rich scent of sage and thyme, picked earlier from my garden, wafted up from the gleaming sauce, loaded with sliced field mushrooms succulent with absorbed cooking juices.

"Doesn't she have any children or grandchildren in the village who could do that for her?" I removed the oven mitts to snip fresh parsley over the fluffy mounds of potato.

"There's a daughter, but she moved away years ago when she got married, and I think she's barely been back since. She was the sort that couldn't wait to get away from the village."

I ladled a generous helping of plump chicken thighs and vegetables on to his plate then mine and set them at our places on the table.

"How sad to have such a rift in her family, especially if she's all alone since her husband died."

"Apart from Bunty. Bunty's all she's got in the world."

My goodness, he was laying it on thick now, but I wasn't going to let him sweettalk me into dog walking. I tried to remember the last time I'd taken a dog for a walk, but I had no recollection of ever doing so.

"Well, I'm not volunteering, if that's what you're hinting at. If you feel that strongly, you can jolly well do it yourself." With any luck, I thought, it might put him off dogs and make him more amenable to Blossom in future.

Waiting for his answer, I narrowed my eyes at him. He played for time, untwisting the cork

39

from the curly blade, folding his Swiss Army knife back up and slipping it into his trouser pocket.

"Oh, you know. Commitment. I couldn't promise to do it every day. You never know when I might have to dash out to make a school delivery or go to a meeting at the library. Besides, if I had a dog, I'd choose something more rugged, something more me." He laid down his fork and flexed his arm muscles. Now we'd reached the crux of the matter. "I wonder whether Tommy's up to the responsibility?"

I took my seat at the table and watched him fill my glass with wine. "I suppose it might take his mind off his sudden craze for birds' eggs. He's already exhausted the farmed birds' eggs available in the village, and we want to keep him off the wild ones. Or might Sina be better?"

I raised my glass and chinked it against his.

"A dachshund is small enough for Sina to control. And it's not as if it'll lead either of

40

them astray, like a bloodhound or a hunting dog."

As we began to tuck into our food, I hoped Hector wouldn't notice the chicken slivers in Blossom's bowl that I'd fished out of the casserole before he arrived.

"You do know what dachshund means, don't you?" I pronounced the two syllables, *dachs* and *hund*, in my best German accent. "Badger hound. There's a reason they're so slender – they're bred to slip into a badger's sett and, er, hound them out."

Hector hesitated, a forkful of chicken halfway to his mouth.

"But Bunty's a lap dog. She wears a pink velvet collar. She's hardly Attila the Hund."

I'd picked the wrong moment to take a mouthful of wine. I had to wait to stop coughing before I replied.

"Tommy often walks Donald's dog, so he's got experience."

Donald is the landlord of The Bluebird, the village pub.

"Good point, Sophie. Well, if you see Tommy before I do, tell him to go and knock on Mrs Shipley's door to volunteer. Then she can stop worrying about Bunty's well-being and concentrate on convalescing. Good, that's sorted then. Now, enough about animals. This evening is meant to be about us."

When he reached a stockinged foot under the table and ran it up my calf, all thoughts of cats and dogs went clean out of my head.

7 The Most Perfect Thing

"Are you going to blow those things so you can keep them?" Billy scratched his stubbly chin in contemplation.

Tommy and Sina had brought their woodpigeons' eggs back into the bookshop, this time in a battered old biscuit tin lined with crumpled toilet paper.

"What, you mean like this?" Lifting an egg delicately to her mouth between finger and thumb, Sina drew in a breath deep enough to puff out her cheeks, before exhaling sharply through pursed lips, as if trying to extinguish birthday cake candles. "What's the point of that? It's not like it's a boiled egg that's too hot to eat."

43

Billy slapped his tweeded thigh, ho-ho-ho-ing so loudly that any small children in the shop might have guessed he played Santa at the school Christmas Fair.

"Bless you, no, girlie, I mean to get the inside out so's the shell keeps fresh. Haven't you ever done that? What about when you're decorating eggs at Easter time?"

Sina shook her head. "Easter eggs don't last long enough in our house to get decorated. We just scoff them right down."

"We finished this year's ages ago," added Tommy.

Billy sighed at the dissolute habits of modern children.

"I'm talking about real eggs. When we were nippers, we used to blow eggs every Easter in our house."

As I set Billy's coffee down in front of him, alongside two small milkshakes that Tommy and Sina had persuaded him to buy for them, I tried to clarify what Billy meant.

44

"You know, by sticking a darning needle in each end, then blowing in the top hole to make the white and the yolk come out the other."

Sina dipped her finger in the frothy top of her milkshake and sucked it clean.

"Oh, that sort of egg blowing. Yes, of course we do that for the children's decorated egg competition at the village show. Mum likes using the eggs' insides for her quiche entry. Should we do that with these too?"

The very thought of quiche made with pigeons' eggs made me clap my hand to my mouth. I made a mental note never to buy quiche at the village show.

Billy chuckled.

"I don't think your ma will be any keener than Sophie on that idea. No, if you're going to keep eggs long-term, you want to ditch the insides. Otherwise, if you drop an old egg, you'll stink the house out. You need to blow them, then give them a good clean inside."

Sina contemplated the size of the egg.

"How on earth am I meant to do that? You couldn't get a scrubbing brush through a hole in an egg. Not even my toothbrush would be small enough."

Billy leaned forward.

"Does your mum keep any brandy in the house? That's what Eggy used to use. He would sneak some out of our granddad's hip flask when he was asleep in his chair and store it in an old medicine bottle under his mattress."

Hector strolled over to the tearoom sink to fetch a glass of tap water. "That's my kind of medicine. But if you ask me, even when it wasn't illegal, collecting birds' eggs must have been an unpleasant and destructive hobby, ridding the eggs of any trace of life and keeping only the dead empty shell. Birdwatching I could understand. At least birds move about, and there's all sorts of interesting behaviour to observe. But if you just want to collect something pretty – and legal – you'd be better off going for stamps."

"Ooh, I love stamps," I said, hoping Tommy might find my enthusiasm infectious. "I used to collect stamps when I was little and have always thought of them as tiny works of art, designed to please a Borrower. I can probably find you some nice old foreign ones to start you off from the letters my Auntie May used to send me on her travels."

May Sayers had been a professional travel writer, quite famous in her heyday. We still sold quite a lot of her books at Hector's House.

When Tommy failed to react, I brought up the topic of walking Bunty, Mrs Shipley's dachshund.

"I'll do it if Mrs Shipley takes that soppy pink collar off," growled Tommy. "I'm not walking a dog that wears one of those."

"You need to keep Bunty's collar on, Tommy, so that you can attach her lead."

Tommy slurped up his milkshake in one long mouthful. "I could train it to walk to heel. I'll bend it to my will."

Hector groaned. "I don't think Mrs Shipley wants her dog's will bent. Besides, I've been reading up about dachshunds in one of our dog books, and apparently you can't train them to walk off the lead. They have a mind of their own and are very determined, doing exactly what they want to do. They think they are a big dog in a small dog's body."

Tommy sat up a little straighter.

"I think Bunty and I are going to get along. Would it be OK if I just disguise its collar?"

"Provided you don't damage it or stop it functioning as a collar. How do you plan to do that?"

Sina swished her ponytail.

"I can lend you one of my hair scrunchies if you like."

Tommy recoiled from the wrinkly band of mauve velvet, then his hand flew to his own collar.

"I know. It can wear my school tie."

I grinned. "Sounds perfect. Just wrap it round Bunty's neck enough times so that it doesn't trail on the ground and trip her up. Dachshunds' legs are very short. And don't wreck your tie, either, or your mum will not be pleased."

Tommy fingered its frayed end. "It's seen worse," he said carelessly.

"That's true," added Sina.

I didn't ask for details.

Over at the trade counter, Hector was checking out a dachshund enthusiasts' YouTube channel.

"You know, dachshunds aren't as soppy as they look, Tommy. As Sophie told me, they were originally bred to hunt badgers in their setts. It says here they're very good at digging. There's a video of one here going at the ground like a meerkat."

Tommy went over to the trade counter to see for himself. "So I could hire it out for digging people's gardens," he said thoughtfully. He reached up to untie his tie and pulled it free of his grubby shirt collar. Holding one end with his hand, he wrapped the full length of the material around his wrist with the other.

I winced, picturing Bunty's slender neck. "Not too tight, Tommy!"

Sina drained her milkshake and went over to join them, so Hector ran the video again.

As soon as the film finished, Hector clicked away from YouTube and the children made for the door, Tommy pausing on the threshold to ask one final question.

"Am I getting paid for walking Bunty?"

Hector passed his hand over his mouth in thought.

"Judy Parkinson never mentioned money. Perhaps she was hoping some kind person would do it as a neighbourly favour. Besides, it's only for a little while until Mrs Shipley is able to walk without sticks. She mustn't risk getting Bunty's lead wrapped round her sticks and pulling her over."

Would virtue be sufficient reward for Tommy? I had faith in his generous nature.

"Fine by me," he said brightly. "I can always find another way to make it pay. Like selling any badgers Bunty kills for me."

Before we could protest, he had slammed the door behind him, leaving the shop in stunned silence.

"Out of the bird's nest, into the badger sett." Hector sounded mournful. "Sophie, tell me we haven't just sent Tommy down a path to a life of environmental crime and prison?"

I scrabbled for words that were honest but reassuring.

"Oh, I don't know. With that attitude, he's just as likely to end up prime minister."

8 Payment in Kind

By the next evening, Tommy's arrangement with Mrs Shipley was a done deal. Shortly before closing time, Tommy strode into Hector's House with a dachshund the colour of butterscotch pattering eagerly alongside him on a conker-brown leather lead. Wrapped three times around Bunty's neck, Tommy's school tie was secured with an elaborate knot. The lead was looped around Tommy's wrist, and he also grasped it tightly with both hands. At least there was no chance of him losing either tie or dog. It was good to see Tommy taking his new responsibilities seriously.

Hector got up from his stool to peer over the trade counter for a better view of Bunty.

"I'm sorry, Tommy, but you can't bring that dog in here. Shop policy: assistance dogs only."

"He's assisting me." Tommy shortened the lead slightly. "He's showing me where he wants to go."

I looked up from mopping the tearoom floor.

"Bunty's a girl's name, Tommy. That dog's a girl."

Tommy frowned. "Just because an old lady puts a pink collar on a dog doesn't make it a girl."

I plunged the mop back into its bucket and strolled over to take a closer look at the little dog. She was awfully cute. It was hard to believe she was a hunter.

"I mean, I know Bun's physically female," Tommy added, "but not in spirit."

"Bun?" Hector's lips twitched at the corners.

Very gently, Tommy applied the toe of his shoe to Bunty's bottom. Immediately she sat

54

down, wagging her little tail at the thought of having pleased her master.

"Bun's what I call him. I don't think he looks like a Bunty. I think he's a boy dog trapped in a girl's body. I'm giving him the chance to express his masculine side. Bun's a brilliant digger, by the way. We haven't caught any badgers yet, but we did find an ace dead rat."

I glanced at Tommy's blazer pockets to check for rat-sized bulges and was relieved to see their misshapen form too small to accommodate rodents.

Hector steered the conversation back on track.

"Anyway, Tommy, the dog's self-identity is immaterial. Bunty's still a dog, and I'm afraid if you're coming into the shop, you'll have to leave her outside."

"But he's thirsty." Tommy stared longingly at the drinks menu on the blackboard. "So am I. We've been walking for nearly two hours."

55

Hector pointed to the shop door. "There's a bowl of water on the pavement outside."

Tommy pulled a disgusted face. "I'm not drinking out of that."

I laughed. "I'm glad to hear it. Goodness knows what you might catch. Anyway, if you've been out that long, you should probably return Bunty to Mrs Shipley. She'll be thinking you've got lost. Or that you've lost Bunty."

Tommy groaned. "I was just in the mood for a milkshake too. A big one, strawberry, with sprinkles."

In spite of the no-dogs-rule, Hector knelt on the floor to stroke Bunty's sleek head.

"Really? Mrs Shipley must be proving a generous employer."

Tommy's mother, raising him and Sina on her own, couldn't afford pocket money.

Tommy frowned. "I'm not sure. She said she'd pay me in kind. What does that mean? Just that she'll be kind to me if I walk Bun for her?" His brow furrowed. "That's all very well, but kindness doesn't buy milkshakes."

56

Hector laughed.

"Make a note of that, Sophie. We should put it on a sign for the tearoom wall."

I was glad of the opportunity to expand Tommy's vocabulary.

"Don't worry, Tommy. What she means is she'll pay you with something other than money. Perhaps in snacks, or she might give you a present. Old people often have material things they don't want, which they're glad to pass on to someone who will appreciate them."

Tommy's eyes widened.

"You mean she might give me her house, like your old auntie gave you hers? No, that would be too much. I'm only walking her dog. Besides, I'm having fun. You're my new best mate, aren't you, Bun?"

Bunty's caramel eyes gazed at him adoringly, her tiny tail wagging as fast as it could. Maybe the dog's affection would be payment enough.

"We're making lots of new friends, too. Have you ever talked to any of those walkers that traipse through the village on the Cotswold Way? They've got to be crazy wanting to do that, but most of them seem all right."

I wondered whether the walkers felt the same way about Tommy. We didn't want him driving tourists out of the village before they'd had the chance to use our shops and the pub. Ramblers make a significant contribution to all village enterprises.

Tommy bent down to straighten Bunty's tie.

"Mrs Shipley does have a lot of stuff in her house, though. That's probably why she's got such a small dog, so it'll fit through the gaps. She's kept all her husband's things, and he died years ago, when I was a little boy. She's even got his overcoat, hat and stick still hanging on a peg in her hall, as if she's expecting him to put them on to go out at any time."

Poor Mrs Shipley. With her daughter out of her life too, she must have been lonely. Perhaps we had done the right thing by sending Tommy in her direction. His vivacious personality must have come like a breath of fresh air into her muddled, stale home. Beneath his outer turmoil, his heart was as warm as a hot water bottle.

Tommy brightened. "I don't suppose Hector's House accepts payment in kind?" Tommy went on.

Hector's resolve weakened.

"I tell you what, how about I pay you commission in kind for any new customers you bring in here that you meet while you're walking Bun on the Cotswold Way?"

Tommy's business instincts kicked in.

"Does it depend on what they buy or on how much they spend? Do they have to buy books, or will drinks and cakes count? What if I bring them in and they don't buy anything? How can I make them buy things?"

"That's my job, and Sophie's. Just lure them in, leaving Bun tied up outside, and we'll do the rest. There'll be a milkshake on the house for you every time you bring someone in, and a cookie if they spend more than ten pounds during their visit."

"On the house?" Tommy looked at me for translation.

"That means free, Tommy."

"Now you're talking my language! I bet I can bring loads of people in, easy peasy."

"That's the spirit!" Hector liked to encourage enterprise. "Just tell them what they want to hear."

Tommy was already on his way, tugging at Bunty's lead so enthusiastically that her front paws lifted right off the ground. He turned round when he reached the door.

"Have you got a toilet they can use?"

I pointed to the WC sign beside the stockroom door.

"Oh, great! I'll start tomorrow, straight after school. See you guys then."

Oozing confidence, Tommy marched out of the shop, Bunty's little paws taking ten steps to every one of his.

Hector got up to shut the door behind Tommy and turned the hanging sign to "Closed". He leaned back against the door for a moment and covered his face with his hands, emitting a low groan.

"Oh, Sophie, what have I done? Tell me I haven't just given licence to every passing walker to come in and use our loo, and promised to fill Tommy's bottomless stomach for the privilege?"

I bit back a smile.

"If you ask our signwriter nicely, maybe he'll add an extra line to the shop fascia: 'Tearoom – Bookshop – Public Convenience'. Although 'WC' would be an easier fit."

As I glanced out of the shop window to see whether anyone was passing by, two small children pressed their noses against the glass, waving shyly at the knitted scarecrow standing at the centre of the window display. I didn't want an audience for our end-of-day routine.

"Come on, Hector, don't be downhearted. Let me cheer you up. Staff meeting in the stock room, right away."

I took his hand to lead him to the small, windowless room. With his spare hand, he flicked off the interior lights before following as obediently as Bunty on her lead.

9 The Pheasant's Egg

"Tommy, I don't want to see any more wild birds' eggs in this shop."

Hector's voice was stern.

Tommy turned to me accusingly. "Did you hear that, Sophie?"

I nearly dropped the tray of empties I was carrying to the dishwasher.

"He means you, Tommy. I haven't been out collecting wild birds' eggs. That was a one-off by my kitten. I've told her off and she won't do it again." If she does, I hope it won't be while Hector is at my cottage. "Besides, how many times do we have to tell you? Collecting wild birds' eggs has been illegal for decades."

Tommy was unmoved. "How do you know this is a wild bird's egg anyway? It might be a quaker's egg, like the one Kate gave me."

"Quail's," I corrected him.

Tommy shrugged. "Quails, quakers, same difference. If it had been down to me to name birds, I'd have done a much better job of it. Anyway, I didn't steal this egg from anywhere. Someone just gave it to me while I was walking Bun."

Hector harrumphed.

"So that dog is an egg magnet now?"

Poor Bunty, her lead tied to the iron loop set into the wall outside the shop, was being tried in her absence.

Tommy was unabashed. "Anyway, I expect you're wondering what type of egg it is. Obviously it's from some sort of bird."

I set down my tray and went over to examine it. The small, glossy green egg reminded me of an olive.

"Actually, Tommy, not all eggs come from birds. Some mammals lay eggs too."

64

Tommy's eyes were as round as a yolk. "No! Really?"

"Yes, the duck-billed platypus and the echidna."

"Are there any of those around Wendlebury?"

Hector looked up from the trade counter.

"You'll have to walk Bunty all the way to Australia to have a chance of finding either of those, Tommy. I'll look your new egg up for you. Sophie, have you seen my *Observer's Book of Birds' Eggs*? I'm sure I left it on the trade counter."

He rummaged in the drawer beneath. Tommy shot me a pleading look, so I came to his rescue.

"Oh, sorry, Hector, while you were busy with a customer the other day, Sina asked me whether she and Tommy could borrow it. I know you're always saying that anyone who doesn't like reading just hasn't found the right book yet. I thought this one might be Tommy's."

Tommy had once told us he thought all books looked alike, in the same breath as asking for a part-time job in the shop.

Tommy continued unabashed. "Anyway, they breed pheasants round here for shooting, don't they? Mum's always complaining about pheasants running out in the lanes in front of the car. Mum says the gamekeepers ought to keep them off the road, same as chicken farmers. So I reckon they don't count as wild birds, so this isn't a wild bird's egg."

Hector remained unconvinced.

"That sounds a bit of a grey area. I'll have to look into that. Besides which, where are all those walkers you were planning to bring me?"

Tommy waved a hand. "Don't worry, it's all under control. Sophie, can you please look after my pheasant's egg while I'm out finding walkers for you? Oh, and you'd better have a banana at the ready for my return."

Before I could ask him why, he had set the egg down in the basket of napkins on the tearoom counter and was heading for the door.

"I think he means for a banana milkshake," said Hector. "I'm glad at least one of us is confident about our little arrangement." He pulled his laptop towards him and poised his hands over the keyboard, ready to start typing.

As Tommy untied Bunty from the metal loop outside the shop, I lingered by the window, gazing out into the spring sunshine. The cloudless sky was the colour of a hedge sparrow's egg. Tommy wasn't the only one who found birds' eggs fascinating. The previous night, I'd dug out Auntie May's old bird book from the shelf in my spare bedroom and had been reading it in bed. I was starting to feel quite the oologist, a word I'd just learned from Auntie May's book.

I turned to Hector. "There shouldn't be any shortage of targets for him in this weather. Not that serious walkers are deterred by bad weather, especially the type that do the whole Cotswold Way for a holiday. But I suspect he'll have a better chance of luring fair-weather walkers into the bookshop than those on a serious mission."

The vicar, who had been quietly browsing the gardening section, came over to sit at a tearoom table. On the empty seat beside him he set his planned purchase, a new organic vegetable manual by the presenter of a Sunday evening gardening programme. After ordering a cream tea, he latched on to our conversation.

"Have you ever thought of putting tea tables on the pavement outside the shop? It might tempt passing walkers to call in, even without Tommy's powers of persuasion."

Hector came over to help himself to an Eccles cake. The only other customer in the bookshop had been standing in the fiction section reading the same novel for about ten minutes, so was the ideal time for Hector to take a break.

At the table next to the vicar, a pair of middle-aged village ladies were enjoying their weekly cream tea and catch-up. Hector called across to them.

"Did you hear that, ladies? Vicar leads walkers into temptation!"

Smiling, the blonde lady topped up their teas with Hector's special cream, a milky liqueur that he brews in the stockroom for his regular customers.

"Hold the front page of the *Gazette*! Does the Bishop know you're now batting for the other side, Vicar?"

The vicar took the ladies' banter in good humour, but I was giving his suggestion serious consideration.

"A park bench might be better than a table and chairs outside the shop. Less of an obstacle for passers-by. We must leave enough space on the pavement for wheelchairs and prams."

After filling a teapot for the vicar, I filled another for Hector and delivered it with a cup and saucer to his favourite table in the corner.

Hector was not convinced. "Walkers might mistake a bench for a free public service, offering a seat to the weary, rather than an incitement to spend money in our shop."

The vicar spread jam evenly on his scone. "Nothing wrong with public service," he returned.

I began wiping a recently vacated table.

"We could put a little plaque on it, to make it clear. Walkers always read plaques on benches to see who they commemorate. Well, I do, anyway."

The grey-haired lady raised her hand for attention. "What if people want to sit on it when your shop's closed?"

Her companion laughed.

"You'd better not put something like 'please wait here to be served'," said her companion. "Or they could be there all night."

The vicar was always practical. "How about 'refreshments available inside the shop – please order at the counter'? Or you could provide a bell to alert you in the kitchen, Sophie?"

"I don't mind taking food and drink out to them, but the whole point is to get them to come into the shop. If they don't buy books, they might need maps. Even a few postcards and stamps would be good."

Hector nodded. "Yes, and once they're in, I can charm them as they pass the trade counter."

The middle-aged ladies looked at each other and giggled. The grey one twiddled a curl around her forefinger.

"Ooh, Hector, you siren!"

Before they could get out of hand, the shop door swung open and in strode Tommy. He held an ancient walking stick up in front of him like a tour guide's umbrella, leading a party of three men in their thirties, all in walking gear.

The vicar clasped his hands as if in prayer.

"Goodness me, it's Moses parting the Red Sea with his staff."

Tommy, with elaborate courtesy, directed his guests to the tearoom table I'd just wiped and helped them off with their backpacks. All three had maps of the Cotswold Way in transparent plastic pockets hanging round their necks, as well as binoculars.

71

Tommy grabbed two extra menus from nearby tables so his party could have one each.

"I highly recommend the banana milkshakes," he advised, before turning to address us. "Sophie, Hector, Vicar, these are my new friends, Graham, David and Stephen." Each raised a hand as he mentioned their name. "They're all brothers." He turned back to the walkers. "Sophie who does the tearoom, and Hector does the books. The vicar doesn't work here, he just does the church." He waved towards the two ladies seated nearby. "And these are some happy customers. Now I will leave you in the capable hands of my colleagues." He gave them a little bow and trudged over to the tearoom counter, where I quickly mixed him a banana milkshake in a takeaway cup.

I heard one of the ladies whisper to the other, "I'd rather be in the capable hands of Hector."

For the first time, I wondered whether the reason they kept coming back each week was because they fancied my boyfriend. I wasn't sure how I felt about that. Placing the milk bottle on the counter a little more heavily than I intended, I decided to water down their cream next time they were in.

10 The Birding Brothers

"Is that charming boy your little brother?" asked Graham, once Tommy had left, slurping his reward up through a straw.

Stephen, the youngest, surreptitiously looked me up and down. "He's hardly going to be her son."

I gritted my teeth. "No, he's just a local teenager who likes to help people."

David nodded.

"He's certainly been helpful to us. He's been telling us all about village life, including the latest gossip." He grinned. I didn't dare ask what that was.

"He was very interesting on the local wildlife, too," said Graham. "Seemed to know the names of all the cows in the field where we met him."

I glanced at Hector for verification, but he was no use, his hand clapped over his mouth to muffle a laugh.

The vicar, ever chivalrous, came to my rescue. "Yes, it's true that the farmers round here give a name to each and every cow. Their herds are not so large as to forbid it."

"Maybe Tommy has been helping the local farmer too," returned Stephen.

I had no idea whether this was true, but said, "That must be it. Now, what can I get you gentlemen?"

One of the ladies leaned towards the brothers. "The scones are very tasty. And you must have a jug of Hector's special cream."

The brothers looked at each other, then Graham, who looked like the eldest, spoke for them all.

"Tea and scones for three please, Sophie, with three jugs of Hector's special cream."

I'm always nervous when strangers find out about the cream. I tried to sound casual.

"You're not planning on driving this evening, are you?"

Clearly puzzled, they shook their heads. They'd understand as soon as they tasted the cream.

While I busied myself behind the tearoom counter, filling tiny stone pots with damson jam, clotted cream and butter, and matching jugs from the unlabelled flagon in the fridge, Hector made light conversation with the brothers. Clocking their binoculars, he soon steered the discussion round to the latest book on British wild birds' eggs, the one that Michael had collected the previous week.

When I eventually brought a heavily laden tray to their table, Graham kindly helped unload the various dishes. David was preoccupied with polishing the lenses of his binoculars with a special cloth, and Stephen was writing in a notebook, adding to what looked like a list of bird species and dates that he'd spotted them.

"Have you seen any interesting birds on your walk today?" I asked, genuinely curious. I hoped they didn't expect me to be as knowledgeable about birds' names as Tommy was about the cows'.

Graham administered the teapot, while Stephen poured a generous helping of cream into each cup.

"No, but we've picked up some great tips from your young assistant. Not that we've seen the particular bird we're looking for just yet, but we're going to take another look before it gets dark, then again in the morning before we set off on the next stage of our walk."

Reluctant to reveal my ignorance, I didn't ask which bird they were seeking.

"Are you staying in the village tonight?"

They began to split their scones and lavish them with toppings. When David took a sip of his tea, his eyes opened wide.

"Mmm, nice tea. Yes, we're staying at The Bluebird tonight."

Graham stirred a spoonful of sugar into his cup. "We're having a bit of fun with our choice of B&Bs. As this is a birdwatching holiday, we've chosen to stay only at pubs with birds' names. Last night we were at The Hen and Feathers."

"Tomorrow, The Guillemot," said Stephen, and they all laughed extravagantly.

Having no idea where either of those pubs were, presumably each a day's walk from Wendlebury Barrow, I smiled politely, then went to attend to the lascivious ladies, now waving to me for their bill.

11 Which Came First?

"A guillemot in Wendlebury Barrow? Surely not?"

Hector laid down the greetings cards he was price-labelling and came over to give me a quick hug and a kiss before the shop opened. I slipped off my jacket and hung it on its usual hook.

"That's what a man outside the village shop just told me. When those birdwatching brothers mentioned The Guillemot yesterday, I thought they were talking about a pub. Guillemots are seabirds. I've seen them in the Outer Hebrides, but we're miles from the coast here. The man who spoke to me just now looked such an expert that I didn't like to point that out to him. He had all the right gear for a serious birdwatcher: khaki field jacket with loads of pockets, a camouflage hat, and a really expensive-looking pair of binoculars around his neck, as well as a camera with an enormous lens. Auntie May would have said he wasn't doing his posture any good."

Hector ambled over to the travel section and pulled an atlas off the shelf.

"The Outer Hebrides, eh? They always sound like a made-up place to me, like Atlantis or Hades."

He opened the atlas at a map of Scotland.

"Don't let my mum hear you say that."

"Why, she's not from the Outer Hebrides, is she? I thought your parents were English."

"Yes, they are, but her dissertation was a study of the evacuation of St Kilda."

"Who was she?"

I sighed. It was hard to believe that Hector, so worldly in so many ways, had never been to Scotland. I went over to put my finger on a tiny dot at the top left corner of his map.

"St Kilda is a little group of islands that are part of the Outer Hebrides, the most remote of them all. It's an extraordinary place. For generations, the locals more or less lived off seabirds like guillemots and gannets, eating the birds and their eggs. They used their oil for lighting and the feathers for bedding."

"A multi-tasking seabird. Impressive."

"But eventually the younger generation decided they'd had enough of the old ways and emigrated to Canada or Australia or America to make new lives for themselves. Inevitably there came a point at which there were no longer enough young, fit people left on St Kilda to maintain their community. So in about 1930, the government took everyone off the island and rehomed them on the mainland."

"I'd have thought they'd be glad to get to civilisation."

"The hustle and bustle of a dirty city after a peaceful island? Not if that's all you know. It must have broken their hearts." Mum would have been proud of me for defending the

83

cultural heritage that she loved so much. "I wouldn't fancy swapping a stone but and ben with a sea view for a Glasgow tenement. After the islanders left St Kilda, they probably never tasted their traditional dishes again. They could hardly pop down to the local chippie for deep-fried guillemot."

"I think they get the odd guillemot on the south coast too," said Hector. "I'm pretty sure Dad's mentioned seeing one in Clevedon. He's quite keen on birds."

Hector's parents had retired to the Somerset seaside town when they transferred their shop to him.

He typed a few words into the search box on his laptop.

"It seems there's a Guillemot Road in Portishead, just up the coast from Clevedon, for what that's worth. Mind you, they've also got a Phoenix Way, so perhaps it doesn't signify. But back to Wendlebury Barrow, what would a guillemot be doing here? Could it have been blown inland by a storm out at sea?"

"I don't know, but there are hordes of birdwatchers up by the village hall who might tell us."

Hector peered past our window display to see for himself.

"So there are. We ought to quickly put any bird books we have in stock in the shop window, just in case they pass by. I might even raid my curiosities collection for any more vintage bird books."

"Actually, they look intent on staying where they are till they get a sighting of the guillemot. But I bet they'd go a bundle for some breakfast rolls and coffee, especially if I offer to deliver them. I'm guessing being a birdwatcher is a lot like being a film extra – 99% sitting around and waiting for something to happen. If there's not much action, regular shots of caffeine will help them stay awake. A few of them are drinking out of thermos flasks, but they won't last long."

Turning his back on the shop window, Hector rubbed his hands together.

"Brilliant, Sophie. This could turn out to be a very lucrative day for Hector's House."

"For Hector's House Tearoom." I slipped my jacket back on. "Credit where it's due, please. While I'm gone, you should give Donald a ring to suggest The Bluebird offers takeaway lunches – sausage and chips, pasties, that sort of thing. I'll go and take their breakfast orders now, then I'll nip back up to grab bread rolls and bacon from Carol at the shop."

"What, no fried egg sandwiches on the menu?"

"I can microwave bacon, but we've no hotplate in the tearoom to fry eggs."

Only when I saw his grin did I realise he was teasing me.

12 Fancy Fanciers

"Did you see all those men in costume on the high street?" As wardrobe mistress for the Wendlebury Players, Carol always has an eye open for costume ideas. "What's that all about? Do you think they're making a television programme?"

I glanced around to make sure none of the birdwatchers were in the village shop.

"I don't think so, Carol. That's how birdwatchers dress. All those pockets are for their birdwatching equipment, and the camouflage colours make it harder for the birds to spot them."

"Well, the camelflage isn't working now. I had no trouble spotting them when they walked past my shop. Maybe birds' eyesight works differently to ours, what with their eyes being at the sides of their heads rather than the front. I shouldn't like that at all." She put a hand to her temple as if to check her eyes hadn't strayed from their usual place. "Anyway, what can I do you for?"

I pulled a cotton shopping bag out of my jacket pocket and shook out its creases.

"I'm going to offer takeaway breakfast rolls to the birdwatchers, that is if you weren't planning to do something like that yourself?"

Although all the village traders always need extra business, we go out of our way not to compete against each other.

"Not at all, my dear, you carry on. I'll still make money from selling you the ingredients while you'll be doing all the work. Buy plenty, and if you have any leftovers, just bring them back for credit, as long as the packets are unopened. I'm not really meant to give refunds on food for hygiene reasons, but as it's you…"

She probably uses that line with everyone in the village, but there was no time to hang about chatting. As I headed to the B shelf to fill my bag with bacon, bread rolls and butter, the doorbell jangled to admit a familiar figure.

"Michael, what a treat to see you again!" Carol flashed her best smile. "Back for another holiday? And look at you, all dolled up like those boys on the high street. All chums together, are you?"

Michael patted some of the many pockets of his buff waistcoat.

"All part of the birdwatching fraternity, anyway. I'm just back for a day trip this time, Carol. As I told Sophie before, I don't usually dash about the country in pursuit of unusual birds, but a twitcher mate of mine who works for the Natural History Museum at Tring messaged me last night to tell me about the Brünnich's guillemot sighted in Wendlebury. He couldn't get away from work to see it for himself, but knowing I'd been here just recently, he thought I might like the excuse for a return visit. So I left a message at my office to book an impromptu day off, jumped in the car, and here I am. Though I confess I was surprised by the nature of the call-out."

My bag now full, I returned to the front of the shop for Carol to tot up the total and add it to the Hector's House account.

Michael smiled at me.

"Hello, Sophie. How nice to see you. You can tell your boss I finished the book he ordered for me when I got back home and I loved it."

He selected an Aero mint chocolate bar from the A shelf behind us.

"Thanks. But why all the excitement about a guillemot? There are thousands of them up in the Scottish Highlands and Islands, where my mum and dad live. It's hardly an endangered species."

"Ah, but this isn't the common guillemot that we usually see on Britain's coast. It's a Brünnich's guillemot whose home turf – or should that be surf? – is in Arctic waters: Iceland, Greenland, Newfoundland in Canada."

Carol started to ring up my purchases on the till. "Brrr, you're making me chilly, even though I'm still wearing my winter woollies. Ne'er cast a sprout till May be out. If I were a broomstick gillymop, I'd prefer the Cotswolds too."

While she fished the Hector's House account card out of her box and wrote down my total spend, I was still mulling over Michael's comments.

"Is it really so different?"

"Ooh, yes, completely different. The Brünnich's guillemot has a white line on its upper mandible."

I had no idea what that meant.

"How did your friend know about it if he's from Tring? That's a couple of hours' drive from here."

Michael handed Carol a pound coin to pay for his chocolate bar.

"Apparently a young man reported a sighting yesterday to some birdwatchers who happened to be walking the Cotswold Way, and they put out an alert on Twitcher."

"A young man, you say?" Not the way I'd usually describe Tommy, but after his show of impeccable courtesy at Hector's House the day before, the birdwatching brothers might.

"Yes. They've posted again this morning to say they were out at the crack of dawn this morning to try to get a sighting, but no luck yet. They were first on the scene before anyone else arrived." He dropped his 20p change into the charity box raising money for the village school library. "Now I'm off to join them. Just popped in here for a belated breakfast on the way. I've had a long drive fuelled only by coffee."

"Dear me, is that a thing now?" Carol glanced down the aisle to her C shelf. "I'd have thought, per gallon, coffee would be more expensive than petrol. Modern technology, eh? But a strapping young fellow like you needs a heartier breakfast than chocolate. Give Sophie ten minutes, and she'll rustle you up a bacon roll."

I appreciated her free advertisement for my services.

"I'm delivering bacon rolls and hot drinks to any of the birders who don't want to leave their look-out."

Michael beamed. "That's great, Sophie, thanks. Can you please bring me a large latte with my roll?"

"Of course," I replied, and headed back to the shop to set to work, leaving Michael to answer Carol's enquiry about his coffee-powered car.

13 Billy and the Dodo

As I entered the bookshop, Hector had just set the sound system to play Vaughan Williams's *The Lark Ascending*.

I was too busy to tell Hector about my conversation with Carol and Michael. Not only did I have the birdwatchers' orders to fulfil and deliver, but more school run mums than usual had come in for morning coffee. They were eager to gossip about the sudden influx of strange men lurking in the village hall car park.

I'd only just got back from delivering the birdwatchers' breakfasts when Billy came in for his customary elevenses.

"What do them tourists want in all that poncey gear?" he grumbled, settling down at his usual table. "I'll have my usual, please, girlie.

My cousin Eggy never needed any of that, and he did all right. More than all right, really. His passion for birds got out of control. That's how we came to fall out."

Hector, shelving a new delivery of books, was listening in.

"Out of control? How can birdwatching get out of control? It's hardly a high-risk sport."

"Ah, well, he didn't just watch them, did he? He took their eggs. And not one or two. He collected dozens. Hundreds, probably."

Setting Billy's coffee down in front of him, I pulled out a chair at the next table and sank down on to it, grateful to be off my feet for the first time that morning.

"I thought you said collecting birds' eggs wasn't illegal when you were kids?"

"Ah, but you don't have to make something illegal to know it's wrong. Even in them days, before everyone was on about saving the planet every five minutes, we weren't daft. We was raised on *Alice in Wonderland*. We knew about dodos."

For a moment I thought he meant there'd been dodos in Wendlebury. If only.

"What I means is, we knew if we took too many eggs from birds' nests, it weren't no good for the birds. One or two eggs would be fine, especially if there was a big clutch of eggs. Eggy used to say the mother bird wouldn't miss one, but I don't think birds was as daft as he made out. Most birds don't lay more than four eggs and most birds have got enough toes to count to four."

He stared into the distance for a moment.

"Birds can be just as clever as people sometimes. Ever heard of the weaver bird, girlie? Proper little craftsmen, they are. I seen them on telly, weaving straws back and forth to make a beauty of a nest, just like a little basket." He lowered his voice reverentially. "It's at times like that I know there's a god. A man couldn't make an animal like that, so it must have been a god that done it."

Sometimes I envy Billy his simple faith.

"So what did Eggy do with all his eggs? Did he keep them in his bedroom, like Tommy?"

When Billy paused to slurp the foam off his cappuccino, I realised how dry my mouth was, so I got up to make myself a coffee, and one for Hector, too.

"Yes, there was box upon box of them in his bedroom, all laid out to look pretty, like little mosaics. I tried to get him to give up and send them to a museum, but he wouldn't part with them, not for nothing, nor would he stop going after more."

"I don't think you'd be allowed to give wild birds' eggs to a museum these days," said Hector, folding flat the cardboard box the delivery had come in. "Not unless they were historic collections with provenance. I was reading up about it online this morning. Any newly collected eggs have to be destroyed. Otherwise it makes a mockery of the ban."

I put my hand to my mouth in dismay. "That would be devastating, both for the collector and for the person whose job it is to smash them up. How terribly sad."

Billy rubbed his chin. "I expect old Eggy's eggs have long since turned to dust. But he was a sad case in other ways, too."

Recognising the overture to one of Billy's long stories, Hector came over to join him. I set our coffees on Billy's table, sat down beside Hector, and nodded to Billy to continue.

"Most of us lads back then would have picked up an egg or two if we came across it in an abandoned nest or on the ground. But boys is boys, and the rest of us never had the staying power to stick at it for long. We'd be on to the next thing next minute, whether it was fishing for tadpoles to grow into frogs, or whittling sticks, or playing marbles. But Eggy had eyes only for his eggs. You see, his old ma was a widow from a young age, and her loneliness was like an anvil around her neck. I never saw her smile. Not surprising when she had to work so hard to raise Eggy and his brother on her own.

"Then one fine spring day, just like today, Eggy found a blackbird's egg on the ground, and he took it home to show his ma. It made her face light up, he told me, so he made her a gift of it, and she put it in a special dish on her dressing table. Soon he was off collecting eggs at every opportunity, in hope of making her smile again."

I frowned. "Surely there can't have been an inexhaustible supply of local wild birds' eggs all year round?"

Billy shook his head.

"That's just it. But there was a market for them in them days. People would do swaps, like they did with cigarette cards, and sell their spares. In some parts of the country, there were even folk who made their living from collecting and selling wild birds' eggs.

"Now, Eggy was out at work by the time he was 14, and for a while he spent all his spare cash buying eggs from such fellows. He used to spend hours arranging them by type, matching them up by their markings, and rearranging the lot each time he got a new one. His ma thought they looked pretty as a picture, and so they did, too."

I pictured the poor boy, not much older than Tommy, playing with his shoeboxes full of treasure. "Maybe he was trying to create a bit of order and control in his uncertain world."

"If he was, it didn't do him any good. Once he was earning a man's wages, he started buying ever more exotic and expensive eggs from dealers. Some cost him a fortune – sometime as much as a week's wages, or at least what he had left over after paying his ma for his keep."

He paused to lick milk froth from his lips.

"It made his ma proud, but I couldn't look at 'em without thinking of all those mother birds coming back to their nests and finding them empty, and one day I told him so. Supposing his ma was a bird, and she came home to find someone had collected him? She wouldn't be smiling then. I don't think he'd

101

ever thought of it that way, and he didn't thank me for suggesting it. We never spoke again after that. I didn't even get an invite to his wedding. Time was, I thought we'd be each other's best man. Not that I ever needed one, as luck would have it."

He drank the last of his coffee, and as he set his empty cup back on its saucer, it was shaking.

"I never did get to make it up with old Eggy, and I regrets it now, even though I know I was in the right."

I reached across the table to put a comforting hand on his.

"It's never too late to make up, especially with family," I said gently.

He laid his other hand on top of mine, its back a network of tiny scars from decades of gardening.

"It is if they're bloody dead, girlie."

I bit my lip. How could I have not realised? Hector came to my rescue.

"Why don't you get Billy another cup of coffee, Sophie?"

Gently I withdrew my hand to take away his empty.

"On the house," added Hector.

14 Whose Dog is it Anyway?

By mid-afternoon, the time the secondary school bus returned to the village, I was having trouble concentrating on listening to Jemima read. She's one of the village children who comes into the shop for coaching after school.

Michael arrived as Jemima, hand in hand with her mother, was leaving the bookshop. Before he could cross the threshold, he was distracted by the sight of Tommy marching up the road with Bunty, her little paws moving so fast they were a blur. This odd couple always made me smile, but Michael's face was creased in concern. He shouted to Tommy across the street.

"Hoi! What are you doing with my gran's dog?"

Tommy, unperturbed, crossed over without looking both ways.

"What you talking about? This isn't your gran's dog. It's Mrs Shipley's."

Michael folded his arms across his chest.

"My gran *is* Mrs Shipley. So what are you doing with her dog?"

Tommy glanced down as if to check whether Bunty had anything to say about the matter, but she just gazed up at him, adoring.

"I'm taking him for a walk, that's what."

Tommy was often perplexed by grown-ups' inability to grasp the obvious.

Michael cleared his throat.

"If you were doing so with Gran's blessing, you'd know Bunty is a girl, not a boy."

Michael stooped to stroke the dog's head, as if she might need reassurance.

"Not when he's out with me, he's not. Don't you know anything about gender fluidity?"

Michael had no answer to that.

"Anyway, Mrs Shipley asked me to walk Bun while she's convoluting, didn't she, Sophie?"

"Convalescing," I translated.

"What she said," Tommy continued. "She can't walk a dog and use sticks at the same time. She's not a juggler."

Michael had the grace to look abashed.

"I'm sorry, I didn't realise. Actually, I've given up on the guillemot now, but before I hit the road home, I was going to pop round to Gran's to see how she's getting on. Shall I walk back with you now?"

Tommy shrugged.

"It's a free country."

Michael would have to work harder to heal Tommy's wounded pride.

"I take it she's paying you?" Michael was saying as they strolled off together in the direction of Mrs Shipley's cottage, Bunty trotting between them.

"In kind," said Tommy.

I was glad he'd remembered the phrase, but after that they were too far away for me to hear any more of their conversation.

**

It was about an hour before closing time when Michael and Tommy returned to Hector's House, this time without Bunty.

"I've just been showing Michael my museum," Tommy announced proudly.

Sina, who was filling in a crossword on a children's activity sheet at the play table, shot Michael a sympathetic look.

"Poor you. It's dire, isn't it? I'm just glad Mum made him move it out of his bedroom and into the shed."

Michael sank down on to a tearoom chair nearest the play table.

"Yes. No. I don't know." He sighed. "I'm sorry, Tommy, I don't mean to be rude. It really is an impressive collection, as my granddad would have been first to agree. But I

thought he'd got rid of it years ago, long before
he died."

Tommy sat down opposite Michael. Sina
got up to stand behind him and started picking
bits of leaf out of his hair.

"What's your dead granddad got to do with
my brother's museum? Sorry he's dead, by the
way."

Michael ran his fingers through his wiry
hair.

"The thing is, Sina, those eggs in your shed
belong to my gran. Or rather, they're from my
late grandfather's collection. I didn't even
know she'd kept them. But it seems Gran has
been giving your brother some eggs from his
collection every time he takes Bunty for a
walk."

"Did your grandpa collect them himself?"
Sina sounded impressed. "And did he have to
go to prison for it?"

Michael wrinkled his nose.

"It wasn't against the law when he was
doing it. Anyway, he gathered some locally, but

when he was older, he bought some too. Did you notice that some have pencil marks on with place names, as well as bird species?"

Tommy did a double take. "Are those place names? I thought they were just the birds' names. Birds have very complicated names, you know. Like the Bempton gwillymot."

Michael's voice fell to almost a whisper.

"Bempton is a place on the north-east coast of England. The Bempton cliffs host vast colonies of guillemots and were once very popular with collectors. The word Bempton on the egg just means that's where it was collected. It's the egg of a common guillemot. The *uria aalge*, to give it its scientific name. As opposed to the *uria iomvia*."

Suddenly things were starting to make sense. "Tommy, did you by any chance tell those walkers you brought in here yesterday afternoon that you'd seen a Brünnich's guillemot in the village?"

Tommy folded his arms. "What I actually said was I liked the shape of the Brünnich's gwillymot's eggs. When they laughed, at first I thought it was because I was saying it wrong. I'd only ever seen the words written down. But then I realised what they were getting so excited about was when I said the word Brünnich. So I let them carry on being excited."

"But you hadn't seen a Brünnich's guillemot in Wendlebury Barrow, had you? Not the actual bird. Just its egg."

Tommy shrugged.

"Egg, bird, bird, egg. Same difference. That's what that old saying is about, isn't it? Which came first, the penguin or the egg?"

"Chicken." Michael's voice was hoarse. "The chicken or the egg."

"I prefer penguins," said Tommy. "Anyway, Hector kept telling me to tell tourists what they want to hear to get them to stay in the village and spend money, so I did. I figured I could make everybody happy."

Michael clapped a hand to his forehead.

"I should have realised it was pretty unlikely that a Brünnich's guillemot would come to Wendlebury. So should my mate in Tring. Oh, Tommy, what a fool's errand you've led us on!"

Tommy slumped forward and sunk his face down on to his folded arms.

"Oh, Tommy, what have you done now?" said Sina, sounding rather proud that he'd created such a to-do.

Michael scraped back his chair and stood up. "So who's going to break it to the crowds that they've wasted their day looking for a non-existent bird?"

Tommy raised his head, face pale as the vanilla meringues on the tearoom counter, and turned to me for support. I was starting to feel guilty myself now. Hector's House had made a lot of money from keeping the birdwatchers fed and watered all day.

Thankfully, a great idea occurred to me.

"I know, Tommy! Why don't you invite them all over to see your museum instead? I bet they've never seen such an extensive egg collection at close hand, and you could allow them to photograph and handle the eggs, which they'd never be allowed to do at a museum. Then after that, I'm afraid you will have to dispose of them responsibly."

Tommy's face fell at the thought of parting with his new treasure. "Does that mean give them back to Mrs Shipley?"

Michael tried to soften the blow.

"Listen, Tommy, a friend of mine works at the Natural History Museum in Tring. They've got a huge historic archive of eggs there, and I can speak to him to see whether they'd be interested in acquiring the whole egg collection – the ones Gran gave you and any she still has at her house. For once, it's a good thing that Gran is such a hoarder because it means she will likely have kept Granddad's collecting records proving his collection predates the ban."

Ever the optimist, Tommy found a new reason to be cheerful.

"Do you think they'll put my name in the display case so everyone knows I donated them?"

"I expect so," said Michael, generously. "Alongside my grandfather's, of course."

Grinning, Tommy pulled Sina's hair. "Do you hear that, Sina? Your big brother is going to be famous. My name will be in a museum."

"Our name, Tommy. They're bound to want to put your surname. Our surname." She threw down her pencil and took her completed crossword to Hector to claim her reward of a wrapped lollipop from the jar on the counter. "Please may I come with you to show those men your eggs, Tommy?"

"I suppose so, but remember, it's my museum. Come on, quick, before they all go home for their tea."

The two children dashed for the door, Michael following slowly behind. I ran to catch up with him, reaching for his arm to delay his departure.

114

"Michael, do you know what your granddad's nickname was when he was young?"

He looked at me quizzically.

"Eggy. Why do you ask?"

That was all I needed to know.

"Do you think you could pop back here after you've visited Tommy's museum? There's someone I'd like you to meet."

"Wouldn't you like to see the collection yourself before I take it away?"

I turned to Hector for permission to abandon my post. He nodded.

As we fell into step on the high street, I began to tell Michael about Billy.

15 At the Museum

Eggy would have been impressed by the good care Tommy had taken during his brief curation of his collection. He had cleared out his dusty old garden shed to create room for the numerous boxes of neatly packed eggs, all the more stunning for the contrast their perfect shells made with the splintering, peeling shelves on which they were now displayed.

The birdwatchers, chattering like sparrows on their way from the hall, fell silent when Tommy flung open the shed door with the showmanship of a circus ringmaster.

"You know this is all highly illegal?" said Graham, but his wide eyes betrayed his admiration.

"Tommy didn't collect these himself," I put in quickly, fearing they might turn on him for decimating the local wild bird population. "It's an old collection, made when it was still legal, by a man long dead. His widow's only just been able to bring herself to part with them, but thanks to this young man, they're now destined for the Natural History Museum at Tring."

"Can you prove their history?" asked a bearded man in a duck-egg blue bobble hat. "You'll need provenance if you don't want them destroyed."

"Oh, yes," I replied quickly. I wasn't sure of that, but I was scared that otherwise the twitchers might take their walking sticks to the eggs and smash them on the spot. Not that they looked violent types. Angry, noisy men probably wouldn't last long as birdwatchers.

Reassured, the twitchers oohed and aahed at the display and took photographs, most of all of the various guillemots' eggs, with their deep creamy glaze, speckled and splashed as a Jackson Pollock painting.

"I don't even mind having spent the day looking for a non-existent Brünnich's guillemot now," said a man in a waxed cap. "It was worth it to see these eggs. Can I just hold the Brünnich's one again, please?"

I texted Hector, who would just have closed the shop for the night: *Fetch Billy and meet Michael and me at The Bluebird at six o'clock.*

Will do, he texted back. *Any clues as to why?*

I decided to save it as a surprise.

Eventually the birdwatchers drifted away, still chattering excitedly. Leaving Tommy and Sina to close up their exhibition and padlock the shed for safekeeping, Michael and I strolled up the high street to the pub.

***

"Eggy Shipley, as I live and breathe!" cried Billy, staring at Michael as we joined him and Hector at their table.

Michael smiled shyly.

"My name's Michael, but Eggy Shipley was my grandfather. I gather you're his cousin and childhood friend."

He reached across the table to shake Billy's wrinkled hand. Neither of them seemed to want to let go.

"Actually, I think we've met before, a week or so ago at Hector's House. I had no idea who you were until Sophie told me just now. I was in the bookshop the day Sina brought in a woodpigeon's egg. Weren't you in the tearoom then?"

"Ah, so I were. But I didn't get a proper look at you then, or I'd have seen the likeness straight away. I don't always bother with me specs. They cost me a lot of money and I don't want to go wearing them out." Billy tapped the breast pocket of his ancient tweed jacket, where he kept his glasses most of the time. "Your voice ain't like his, mind. You're all posh, not like old Eggy. That father of yours always did give himself airs and graces. That's why your ma married him. Couldn't wait to leave the village, she couldn't. If your ma wanted to see her, Eggy had to drive her to Bristol himself. Not that he can do that anymore, God rest his soul."

Billy nodded acknowledgement before taking a pull from his pint of cider. "Hector here has been telling me of the mischief young Tommy has been causing with your granddad's egg collection. I didn't even know she'd still got 'em."

"Apparently they were hidden in the loft," I explained. "Tommy told me she sent him up into the loft to bring them down after he'd told her about his plan to make an egg collection. She must have decided that he'd be a fitting trustee for Eggy's collection."

Michael looked hurt.

"Why not me? She must know I'm interested in birds. She saw the book I bought from your shop when I was staying with her."

Billy leaned forward.

"Did you volunteer to walk her dog every day out of the kindness of your heart? Did you

121

do her shopping? Do odd jobs round her house? Sit and listen to her stories? Or just sit and say nothing when she needed it, just for company? That's what that boy's been doing, Hector tells me."

Michael stared down at the table. "I thought just coming to see her was good enough, considering my parents had ignored her for years. But it wasn't, was it? I didn't even take her dog for a walk. I just let it out into the garden to do its business."

Michael stared into the glass of wine Hector had poured for him. "I tell you what, why don't I slip Tommy a few quid to keep walking Bunty till Gran's better?"

"A couple of pounds per walk would be a start," said Hector. "He takes her out for hours at a time. But I honestly think he'd keep doing it anyway. For all his faults, Tommy lives to help people." Michael nodded, chastened, as Hector continued. "And I think removing those eggs to the museum would be a good idea to take them out of harm's way."

I put my arm through Hector's in solidarity.

"Best tell her it's a loan, so she doesn't feel his eggs have gone forever," I suggested. "If she misses them, you could always take her to see them on display in the museum.""

"If they display them," put in Hector, ever practical. "Museums seldom display all their collection at once. Many items are kept in storage away from the public eye."

Michael waved a hand dismissively.

"I doubt she'd want to visit the museum. She seldom leaves the village anyway."

I exchanged glances with Hector. I knew from my own experience how restrictive village life could be for anyone who didn't drive. Hector had been on at me for a while to take driving lessons.

"I bet she'd go out more often if someone offered to take her in their car. There aren't many buses, and they don't go very far."

"Ah," said Michael, my hint sinking in. "Yes, I could do that. I don't see why not. It would be easy."

"It would make such a difference to her."

"You can take me as well if you like," said Billy. He had been sitting quietly just looking at Michael, but I guessed he was still seeing his old pal, Eggy. "You're not the only one to be feeling bad now, son. My row was with Eggy, not Vi. I should have looked out for her after Eggy passed away. I used to like old Vi when we were youngsters. Might have married her myself if Eggy hadn't got to her first."

I spluttered into my glass of wine. I wondered what Mrs Shipley might have to say to that idea. Hector laid a hand on my thigh.

"Now, why don't we leave Billy and Michael to get better acquainted? They've got a lot of lost time to make up for. A lifetime, in Michael's case, of not knowing his grandfather's cousin."

"His grandfather's favourite cousin and best boyhood friend," added Billy. "Me and Eggy was thick as thieves till we fell out over the egg business."

Michael's eyes glistened.

"That would be wonderful. Thank you, Sophie, thank you, Hector, for making this possible."

I grinned.

"Thank Tommy, I think. And his guillemots."

16 Nesting Instincts

As it turned out, Mrs Shipley was able to furnish the necessary paperwork to verify the eggs were collected prior to the ban. Eggy, always meticulous, had kept a detailed journal of the eggs he'd found locally as well as his purchases from further afield. The Tring Museum's curators were thrilled to receive an egg collection that they would not be obliged to destroy.

Michael's visits to his grandmother have become more and more frequent and focus on her needs rather than his, which are chiefly companionship and a sympathetic ear to her reminiscences. It must be heartening for her to get to know better a man who is, as Billy said, the image of her late husband. Michael brought photos of a young Eggy to the shop to demonstrate the family resemblance. Her husband may be long gone, but his genes go on.

Michael even helped his gran declutter her house, a process that Tommy had unwittingly begun when he accepted Eggy's eggs. Once Mrs Shipley's cottage was tidier, Michael persuaded his mother, Mrs Shipley's daughter, Sheila, to visit, along with her husband, Philip. Philip installed useful handrails and other aids to make the cottage safer and more comfortable for the frail old lady, who had for years been living in fear of tripping over her strewn possessions. Now she can relax and enjoy each day as it comes.

Tommy continues to walk Bunty every day, and although Michael pays him in cash, Mrs Shipley still presses the odd gift upon him. Tommy has become particularly fond of Eggy's old trilby. He'd already had the walking stick from the hallstand, which he'd used to lead the birdwatching brothers into Hector's

House. Mrs Shipley made a gift of the overcoat to Billy, who wears it every day, even when the weather is far too warm for it. Eggy's peg is now free for the coats of visitors.

Mrs Shipley's regular visitors now include Sina, who, intrigued by the egg saga, wanted to meet her brother's benefactor for herself. Sheila was the Shipleys' only child and Michael their only grandchild, so Mrs Shipley had never had a granddaughter. She and Sina hit it off famously, and Sina can now be seen parading about the village in a huge black silk shawl embroidered with cerise roses, which once belonged to Mrs Shipley's mother.

Sina's interest in wild birds' eggs was easily displaced, thanks to a book Hector found in his curiosities collection: an illustrated history of Fabergé eggs, those lavishly decorated ornaments favoured by the Russian tsars.

"Why would anyone bother with ordinary old eggs when there are these in the world?" she exclaimed as she showed her favourite page to the vicar in the tearoom.

"Gild not the lily," murmured the vicar, but his wise words were lost on Sina, who has taken to decorating hens' eggs from her mother's pantry. Their family must be eating a lot of quiches these days.

Tommy, meanwhile, has transferred his allegiance to fossils, with the help of a few specimens once owned by Eggy, given to him by Mrs Shipley.

"Although I don't see why I'm allowed to collect these when dinosaurs are extinct, but wild birds aren't," says Tommy, with his unique logic. But at least it means he has something else to fill his shed museum.

Mrs Shipley's son-in-law Philip also found a way to thank Tommy. When he and Sina happened upon Philip one Sunday when he was repairing Mrs Shipley's front garden gate, they fell into a conversation about woodwork, each taking a turn with some of Philip's tools. Before long, the children persuaded Philip to give them a carpentry lesson, of which the fruit was a small wooden nesting box. Philip's other favourite hobby is pyrography, and together Tommy and Sina burned an inscription on the nestbox in shaky capital letters: "For Eggy". I wouldn't normally advocate putting fire and Tommy together, but in this case only good came of it.

The vicar suggested they affix the nest box to a tree in the churchyard near Eggy's grave. Mrs Shipley, now walking with just one stick, came down to the churchyard to witness the vicar bless the nest box as Billy nailed it in place.

***

It was a few weeks before I could bring myself to eat eggs again. Then I decided to make a Spanish omelette to share with Hector one evening after work. I was just about to start slicing the peppers when he arrived at my cottage. As I let him in, I could hear a strange strangulated noise emanating from my garden:

Blossom's "Aren't I clever? I've caught something" cry.

"Tea won't be ready for a while," I said quickly, taking Hector by the hand and leading him to the sofa. "Why don't you relax here for a bit and I'll fetch you a drink?"

To my relief, he obeyed. Settling back, he kicked off his shoes and put his feet up on Auntie May's old Moroccan leather pouffe. (How she got that back in her suitcase from her North Africa tour, I'll never know.)

Then I dashed to the kitchen window and peered out just in time to see Blossom dragging a dead sparrow towards the cat flap. With trembling hands, I locked the cat flap to keep her out, cracked an egg into my mixing bowl and let out an exaggerated groan of dismay.

Then I sauntered back into my front room and lowered myself on to Hector's lap, looping my arm around his neck.

"Oh dear, Hector, I'm terribly sorry. I'm afraid I can't rustle up the Spanish omelette after all. Would you mind awfully if we went to the pub for supper instead?"

"Fine by me, sweetheart," he replied, slipping his arms around my waist. "But why?"

I smiled as innocently as I could.

"The eggs are off."

THANK YOU

*If you enjoyed reading this book,
you might like to spread the word to other readers
by leaving a brief review online –
or just tell your friends!
Thank you.*

FOR A FREE EBOOK

Join Debbie Young's Readers' Club
at her website
www.authordebbieyoung.com
and you will be sent a link
to claim your free copy of
The Pride of Peacocks,
another entertaining short novella
about Sophie Sayers and friends.

You will also receive in your inbox
the latest information about
Debbie Young's books and events.

Also by Debbie Young

Sophie Sayers Village Mysteries (novels)
Best Murder in Show (1)
Trick or Murder? (2)
Murder in the Manger (3)
Murder by the Book (4)
Springtime for Murder (5)
Murder Your Darlings (6)
Coming soon: *Murder Lost and Found (7)*

**Tales from Wendlebury Barrow
(short novellas)**
The Pride of Peacocks
(ebook exclusively available to members of
Debbie Young's Readers' Club at
www.authordebbieyoung.com)
The Natter of Knitters

Staffroom at St Bride's Mysteries (novels)
Secrets at St Bride's (1)
Stranger at St Bride's (2)
Coming soon: *Scandal at St Bride's (3)*

Acknowledgements

Thanks to Bristol Museum and Art Gallery for hosting the provocative exhibition, Natural Selection in which artist Andy Holden and ornithologist Peter Holden explored the wonder of birds, nests and eggs. I highly recommend their book, *A Social History of Egg Collecting*.

I will never look at an egg in the same way again after reading Tim Birkhead's fascinating book, *The Most Perfect Thing Inside (and Outside) a Bird's Egg*.

Alex Horne's *Birdwatchingwatching* provided me with interesting insights into the minds of birders and twitchers alike. This topic first intrigued me when I lived next door to avid birdwatcher David Spencer as a student at the University of York – thanks, Dave!

I'm grateful to the Natural History Museum at Tring for allowing me to reference them in my story. It's a wonderful museum with an interesting heritage and well worth a visit.

Thanks to author Lorna Fergusson for her advice about the impact of a hip replacement on Mrs Shipley's capacity to take her dog for a walk.

With gratitude, as ever, to my fabulous editor Alison Jack, proofreader Dan Gooding, cover designer Rachel Lawston, and technical advisor Paul Lawston for his specialist knowledge of birds and birdwatchers.

Debbie Young

Lightning Source UK Ltd.
Milton Keynes UK
UKHW011836180521
383947UK00001B/292